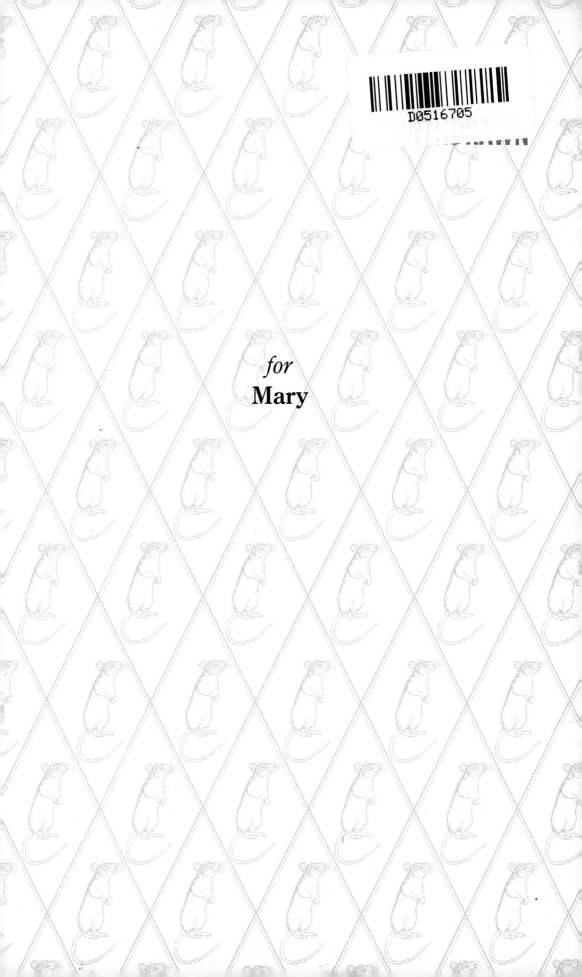

for
Mary

MIKE RICHARDSON • *publisher*

RANDY STRADLEY & DICK HANSOM • *series editors*

LYNN ADAIR • *collection editor*

MICKIE VILLA • *collection designer*

BRIAN GOGOLIN • *art director*

This book collects issues one through four of the Dark Horse comic-book series
The Tale of One Bad Rat.

Published by
Dark Horse Comics, Inc.
10956 SE Main Street
Milwaukie, OR 97222
www.darkhorse.com

To find a comics shop in your area, call the Comic Shop Locator Service toll-free at 1-888-266-4226

First edition: October 1995
ISBN:1-56971-077-5

2 4 6 8 10 9 7 5 3

Printed in China

The Tale of One Bad Rat

by

BRYAN TALBOT

Dark Horse Comics®

THE RAT'S WHISKERS

THERE have been rats in Bryan Talbot's kitchen for longer than I care to remember. I don't mean the kind that scratch around under the floorboards, dodging traps and ignoring poison and finally being dispatched by a couple of council workers with a quick eye and a cricket bat; Bryan's rats have been bright-eyed little charmers with their own immaculate quarters and a taste for boiled rice and chapati.

Their owner has become well acquainted with their ways, too. Very few visitors can have left the house without concluding that, over the years, rats have had a pretty one-sided press. Vermin, plague-bearers, traditional objects of terror; rats, like wolves, have been forced to carry a certain burden of the human imagination. When a rat dives across the path of someone out walking and surprises them, it's never a rat of normal size. In the retelling, it's always at least the size of a cat. A squirrel on the lawn is something to smile at. But stick it on all fours and shave its tail, and there's an instant pucker-factor.

Ever since we lived in caves, we've had to demonise *something* out there; and after a while, it's as if the demons are the only truth we can know. We're born into a world that's full of such received ideas, automatic ways of seeing things, and they surround us as we grow. They're hard to question; the world tends to resist having its assumptions challenged, and its non-conformist thinkers have been given a hard time throughout history. It's much easier to accept the general line. Do otherwise, and you're a rebel, you're weird . . . and the weird and rebellious are always suspect.

So how do you handle it, then, if you happen to be brought up in an atmosphere of certainty that the demon is *you*?

That's how it can be when you're a child if the adults in your life can't be relied upon, and they seem to get some consolation out of projecting their inadequacies onto you. I don't know why it's such a human trait, to react to feeling badly by looking for someone weaker, that you can make feel worse, but there it is. In every generation, there's this urge among a number to damage the next. Sometimes because it makes them feel better. Sometimes just because they can.

And children, of course, believe what they're told. They're credulous in the most open way because they simply haven't the data to know otherwise. Make them think that they're guilty, and they'll wonder what it was they did. Let them think they're worthless, and they'll assume it must be a true valuation.

Bad rats, all.

When a soul's been starved in this way and kept in darkness, its only hope lies in making its own journey out of there. And when the darkness is your entire world, even starting such a journey requires a faith in yourself that can be very hard to muster.

What you are about to read is the tale of such a journey. Picked from among countless numbers, this is *The Tale of One Bad Rat*.

Watching this book as it has moved toward its final form has been rather like seeing the offspring of a close friend growing up and heading out into the world. You feel as if you can share a little bit of the glow of satisfaction while knowing full well that you didn't do a single stroke of all the hard work that was required. I was, Bryan reckons, about the third person ever to hear him recount the story that was to become the graphic novel you now hold. We were driving back from a joint signing somewhere at the other end of the country, and he wanted to tell it as a way of getting it clear in his own mind.

Since then, I've witnessed the long process of development, the phenomenal concentration, the research, the dedication, and the genuine sacrifice that were to go into the creation of the work you're about to enter. More than one of those small house guests came and went during the process; life is short, but even a good rat's life is shorter than most.

You, of course, will see none of this. You'll see only the *Tale*.

Which is exactly the way it should be.

STEPHEN GALLAGHER
author of *Red, Red Robin*
and *Nightmare, With Angel* & co.

TOWN

Once upon a time, there was a very bad rat...

ROAD

HOMELESS
+ HUNGRY
PLEASE
HELP

NOW WE'VE GOT ENOUGH MONEY TO GET A BITE TO...

HULLO.

MY NAME'S JEREMY.

W-WHAT DO YOU WANT? GO AWAY.

YOU'RE ASKING FOR HELP. I WANT TO HELP YOU.

COME WITH ME.

N-NO. WHERE? WHAT DO YOU WANT?

JESUS CHRIST LOVES SINNERS.

COME WITH ME TO THE SUNSHINE HOSTEL. YOU'LL GET A HOT MEAL AND A BED FOR THE NIGHT.

JESUS LOVES YOU. OPEN YOUR HEART TO HIM.

HE DIED FOR YOU. HE DIED ON A CRUEL CROSS, TAKING THE PUNISHMENT YOU DESERVE FOR YOUR SINS.

MY... SINS...?

PLEASE... GO AWAY.

DENY THE DEVIL; LISTEN TO ME.

"YOU SHALL KNOW THE TRUTH AND THE TRUTH SHALL SET YOU FREE." AND THE TRUTH IS JESUS LOVES...

AAAAH! DON'T TOUCH ME!!

OOOOF!

HIYA, KIDDER.

WHAT'S YER NAME THEN?

HELEN.

NICE T'MEECHA. MINE'S LUCINDA.

NOT SEEN YER ROUND 'ERE BEFORE. YOU'RE A RUNAWAY, ARNCHA?

HOW LONG YER BEEN IN LONDON?

ER... ABOUT A MONTH. SINCE CHRISTMAS.

'EY, HOW WOULD YER LIKE T'MAKE SOME MONEY? DEAD GOOD MONEY IF YER WORK 'ARD. AN' A NICE ROOM. WOULD YER LIKE THAT, 'EY?

'COURSE. BUT WHAT...

CALL ME LUCY.

I STARTED LIKE THAT, Y'KNOW. 'OMELESS LIKE, NO MATES, MILES AWAY FROM 'OME. I'M A SCOUSER.

GETAWAY.

SHURRUP, YOU.

OUR BOSS IS LOOKIN' FOR GIRLS LIKE YOU. YOU'D BE GREAT, LUV. SPRAY YER 'AIR BACK... SOME MAKE-UP AN' NICE CLOTHES...

LOTS O' MEN'LL FANCY YOU.

YOU MEAN... YOU'RE PROSTITUTES!?

STOP THIEF!

⸴COUGH COUGH COUGH⸴ ANY SIGN, BEN?

NAAH. LOST 'IM.

Y'SHOULD LAY OFF THAT *CRACK*, MUN. LET'S HAVE A *SKEG* AT THAT WATCH THEN.

EH, IT'S *CANNY*, THAT.

WOAH! WHAT'S THAT?!

IT'S A RAT.

'EY! 'EY! LISTEN...

"...YOU...DIRTY... RAT...YOU KILLED MY BROTHER!" HA HA HA!

Y'EVER SEE THAT FILM, WILLARD?

NO.

THERE WAS A RAT CALLED BEN IN THAT, THE *BOSS* RAT, LIKE.

SHIT! THERE'S A COUPLA HUNDRED QUID HERE! RICH BASTARD! AN' CREDIT CARDS AN' STUFF...

DUMP THE CARDS. THEY'LL BE *HOT* BY TOMORROW, MUN.

C'MON PET! THE FOOD'S ON US. LOOKS LIKE YOU COULD DO WITH SOME *BAIT*, LIKE.

HELEN ⸴SNIFF⸴

Y'WHAT?

MY NAME'S HELEN.

GOD. I'M STUFFED!

⁑BUUURP⁑

YOU 'AD ENOUGH, PET?

HELEN. YES.

YEAH. SORRY, LIKE. HELEN.

EVERYTHING OKAY, GENTLEMEN?

YEAH, CHEERS BABU, GREAT MUN. MAGIC.

ER... ANOTHER ROUND O' LAGER AN' 'ALF A BITTER FOR THE LASS.

'EY, Y'BEST NOT LET 'IM SEE THE RAT, LIKE. 'E'LL DO 'IS NUT.

⁑CHOO⁑

LOOK, 'AVE THE SCARF— IT'LL KEEP YOU WARM LIKE. I THINK IT'S SILK.

NO. SMELLS OF HIM. I DON'T WANT IT.

Y'NEED TO KEEP WARM. Y'GOT A BAD COLD THERE. WHERE Y' STOPPIN'?

NOWHERE, REALLY. WELL, I'VE GOT A CARDBOARD BOX STASHED...

HOMELESS, ARE Y'? I WAS FOR A BIT, WHEN I FIRST CAME DOON FROM NEWCASTLE, LIKE.

LOOK, WE'RE ALL IN THIS SQUAT LIKE, IN KENSINGTON. COME AN' STOP WITH US. THERE'S PLENTY ROOM.

UH, NO I ⁑SNIFF⁑ UH ...NO. THANKS.

IT'S A GEET BIG PLACE. GOT TEN BEDROOMS, MUN.

Y'COULD HAVE A ROOM ALL TO YOUR-SELF LIKE.

WHAT DO YOU THINK, RATSO?

SHOULD I TRUST THEM?

I NEVER DO TRUST ANYBODY. I WISH I COULD.

⟨PAAARP⟩

BEN DREW A MAP ON THIS FAG PACKET.

IT WOULD BE NICE TO HAVE A ROOM, TO BE DRY AND WARM...

DON'T WANT TO GET TOO CLOSE TO PEOPLE.

SOMETIMES IT SEEMS AS IF THEY CAN SEE RIGHT INSIDE MY EYES... AS IF THEY CAN TELL, JUST BY LOOKING...

...THAT I'M DIFFERENT.

SOMETIMES I FEEL LIKE I'M FROM ANOTHER PLANET.

FINISH YOUR NAAN BREAD, RAT. ⟨SNIFF⟩ I WANT TO SLEEP.

BEATRIX POTTER
Writer and Artist
1866 to 1943
Lived in a house on this site from 1866 to...
...TEL... THE BOLTONS ASSOCIATION, THE BEATRIX POTTER SOCIETY AND FREDERICK WARNE &...

"MY UNLOVED BIRTHPLACE".

AND, JUST ACROSS THE ROAD...

THAT'S THE ONE, RAT. MIDDLE ONE OF THE THREE FOR SALE. WE'VE GOT TO SNEAK ROUND THE BACK.

...TEN...ELEVEN... TWELVE. THIS IS IT. THERE'S SUPPOSED TO BE A LOOSE BOARD...

WHAT...

WA-HEY! SEE WHAT I GOT YA!

GORRIT OFF A SKIP.

Y'GET A BETTER CLASS O' RUBBISH IN KENSINGTON, Y'KNOW.

OH, WOW. THAT'S INCREDIBLE.

OKAY OVER HERE?

UH, YEAH. THANKS. A LOT.

'EY, WHAT'S THAT Y'DOIN', EH?

OH, NOTHING...

'EY, THEY'RE GEET GOOD, THEY ARE. Y'DIDN'T TELL US YOU COULD DRAW, LIKE.

NO, PLEASE DON'T LOOK. THEY'RE ONLY COPIES.

I'VE COPIED DOZENS OF BEATRIX POTTER ILLUSTRATIONS. I... ENJOY IT.

"THE TALE O' TWO BAD MICE"! I REMEMBER THIS FROM INFANT SCHOOL!

'EY, I'M AN ARTISTE TOO, Y'KNOW. A MUSICIAN, LIKE.

IS IT YOU I CAN HEAR PLAYING THE GUITAR EVERY NIGHT?

AYE, THAT'S ME. WRITE ME OWN SONGS AN' ALL. I'M GOIN' TO BE *MEGA* ONE DAY. BIG ROCK STAR, LIKE.

I'M ONLY BUSKIN' RIGHT NOW. IT'S GOOD TRAININ', LIKE, BUT SOME- DAY I'M GOIN' TO GET A BAND TOGETHER.

Y'DON'T PLAY ANYTHIN', DO YA?

UH-HUH.

EH... HELEN...

DO Y'LIKE IT HERE?

'COURSE. IT'S BETTER THAN THE CARDBOARD BOX.

NO COMPLAINTS, LIKE?

WELL... HOT WATER WOULD BE NICE. NOT HAD A BATH SINCE I LEFT HOME. WHY?

IT'S JUST THAT... WELL, SOME OF THE OTHERS THINK THAT YOU'RE *STUCK UP*, Y'KNOW, Y'DIVN'T LIKE 'EM OR SOMMAT.

OH.

I MEAN, YOU'VE BEEN HERE A *MONTH* AN' WE'VE HARDLY SEEN YOU. YOU'RE EITHER OUT BEGGIN', LIKE, OR UP HERE ON THE THIRD FLOOR.

I'M SORRY.

NAAH. Y'DON'T HAVE TO BE SORRY, PET. LOOK, ALL I'M SAYIN' IS WHY DON'T Y'COME *DOWNSTAIRS* IN THE EVENIN' FOR A BIT, Y'KNOW. BE *FRIENDLY*, LIKE...

UH... YEAH. OKAY.

WHAT, *TONIGHT*, LIKE?

IF YOU WANT.

EXCELLENT, MUN!

YOU'LL HAVE TO STAY HERE, RAT. I'M GOING SOCIALISING AND THEY'VE GOT CATS DOWNSTAIRS.

HELEN?

Y'ALRIGHT, PET? HAWAY IN, MUN.

D'YOU FANCY SOME CIDER?

UH... NO. TA.

'EY, PETE! SHOW 'ELEN THAT RAG, MUN!

OH YEAH! COOL! 'AVE A BUTCHERS!

S'THAT OLD FART, INNIT?

OH!

WE NEED LAW AND ORDER

"SIR NOEL TOD"! 'E'S ONLY A BLOODY M.P., INN'E! HA HA HA!

DIRTY OWD TOSSER.

S'A GOOD JOB WE COME ALONG WHEN WE DID, 'EY?

B-BEATRIX POTTER USED TO COPY OTHER P-PEOPLE'S STUFF WHEN SHE WAS A TEENAGER. W-WALTER CRANE... GREENAWAY... CALDECOTT...

MAMA MIA! CALL HER AN ARTIST? GET REAL!

VELLY SOLLY MISSY! REAL ARTISTS NOT PAINT FLUFFY BUNNIES! MERDE!

KNOCK IT OFF, PICASSO. NO NEED T'GET SARKY, MUN.

'E ALWAYS TALKS LIKE THAT. TAKE NO NOTICE, PET.

MEIN GOTT! I HAFF NO TIME FOR ALL DIS! I HAFF VERK TO DO! REAL VERK!

NOW I GO CLEANIN' WINDERS TO EARN AN' HONEST BOB FOR A NOSY PARKER IT'S AN INTERESTIN' JOB...

WHY DON'T YOU DRAW YOUR OWN PICTURES, 'STEAD OF RIPPIN' OTHER PEOPLE OFF?

I ...UH... I DON'T KNOW...

WHA? HELEN?

UH HUH

UH HUH HUH

UH HUH HUH

HUH UH UHN

AAAWWW HUH UH UHUH ...

UHN...B... BASTARD...YOU DON'T LOVE ME...UH... N-NOBODY D-DOES... UHUH...

I DO, MUM.

I DIDN'T MEAN YOU, STUPID!! GET BACK TO BED! PRYING LITTLE SOD!

GO AWAY! I DON'T WANT YOU!

I NEVER WANTED YOU!

SHEEE. I'M KNACKERED, ME. I'VE 'AD ENOUGH FOR TODAY.

HOWAY, IT'S A LONG WALK BACK. WE'LL STOP FOR A PIZZA OR SOMMAT IN CHELSEA ON THE WAY.

MM. I'M HUNGRY. AND MY FEET ARE COLD.

I'M NOT SURPRISED IN THOSE THINGS. THE SOLES ARE FALLIN' OFF AN' ALL.

WE'LL CUT THROUGH THE PARK.

Y'KNOW, THE OTHER NIGHT... Y' SHOULDN'T MIND BERTRAM. E'S LIKE THAT WITH ANY BUGGER. TOTAL HEAD THE BALL, LIKE.

'E READ ABOUT SALVADOR DALI, LIKE, Y'KNOW, SPEAKIN' IN DIFFERENT LANGUAGES ALL THE TIME. 'E THOUGHT IT WAS REAL NEAT, LIKE.

THING IS 'E CAN ONLY SPEAK ENGLISH.

OH, BEN.

THE STARS!

FWOARR! Y'DIVN'T USUALLY SEE 'EM THAT CLEAR IN THE CITY. GREAT, MUN.

JUST LOOK AT IT ALL.

IT'S ENDLESS.

WHAT DO WE MATTER, BEN? WHAT DO WE MATTER?

THAT'S WHAT IT IS, LAZY RAT. I'M WORTHLESS.

THAT'S WHY I COPY ILLUSTRATIONS...

...WHO'D BE INTERESTED IN ANYTHING I DID?

I WOULD, PET.

BEN!?

GOT YOU A PREZZY.

WHAT...

A PAIR O' DOCS. SMALL. SHOULD FIT YOU.

OOOF!

I TRADED FOR 'EM, LIKE.

AW, BEN. THAT'S REALLY KIND OF YOU. YOU SHOULDN'T...

Y'GOIN' T' GIVE US A KISS FOR 'EM, THEN?

ARE YOU DRUNK?

S'ONLY A BIT O' CIDER, LIKE.

Y'GOIN' T' GIVE US A KISS OR WHAT?

WELL... OKAY.

NAA, MUN...

I... I'M SORRY, PET.

I REALLY AM.

ARE Y'... ARE Y' STILL A *VIRGIN*, LIKE?

IT'S NOT *THAT*.

DON'T THINK I'M NOT GRATEFUL, BEN.

YOU'VE BEEN KIND TO ME. YOU'VE SHOWN ME *REAL* FRIENDSHIP. IT'S JUST THAT...

I CAN'T BEAR TO BE *TOUCHED*.

I'M NOT *READY* TO BE TOUCHED. IT MAKES ME *SICK* TO BE TOUCHED.

PLEASE DON'T ASK ME TO TALK ABOUT IT. I'M SORRY.

HELLO, LITTLE RAT.

BEEN EXPLORING?

SHE'S GONE INTO "WASHING MODE". SHE DOES THIS ABOUT EVERY FIFTEEN MINUTES.

AN' FOLKS THINK RATS ARE DIRTY, LIKE.

THEY'RE CLEANER THAN PEOPLE! NO, THEY'VE JUST HAD A REALLY BAD PRESS.

THEY WERE A SYMBOL OF LUCK IN ANCIENT ROME. IN JAPAN THEY WERE THE MESSENGERS OF THE GODS AND IN CHINA A SYMBOL OF PROSPERITY.

Y'KNOW, IT'S BEEN ESTIMATED THAT THE NUMBER OF RATS ON THE PLANET ALWAYS CORRESPONDS TO THE HUMAN POPULATION.

YEAH? WELL, THEY ALWAYS LIVE WHERE THERE'S PEOPLE, EH?

THAT'S HOW THEY LIVE. PART OF THE ECO-SYSTEM. PEOPLE DON'T REALIZE. THEY THINK RATS ARE VICIOUS. BUT THEY'RE NOT PREDATORS, THEY'RE SCAVENGERS. BORN SURVIVORS.

I THOUGHT THEY ATTACKED PEOPLE. BIT YOU, LIKE.

ONLY IF YOU'RE STUPID ENOUGH TO TRY AN' GRAB HOLD OF A WILD ONE!

THEY'RE INTELLIGENT. THERE'S A BIG DIFFERENCE IN PROPORTION OF BRAIN SIZE BETWEEN RATS AND THINGS LIKE GERBILS AND HAMSTERS.

AND THEY'RE SOCIAL CREATURES. IN THE TRENCHES IN WORLD WAR ONE, SOLDIERS SOMETIMES KEPT THEM IN THEIR UNIFORMS AS PETS. THEY... WHAT'S UP?

HEH HEH! Y'BUGGER!

Y'CAN TALK THE BACK LEGS OFF A DONKEY WHEN Y'GET GANNIN'! THAT'S THE *MOST* I'VE EVER HEARD YOU SAY, MUN!

WELL... I-I'VE JUST READ *A LOT* ABOUT RATS...

HOW LONG Y'HAD *THAT* ONE, LIKE?

TWO YEARS. THAT'S QUITE *OLD* FOR A RAT.

SHE'S SWEET. I DON'T REALLY LIKE LEAVING HER IN THE BOX DURING THE DAY, BUT I *SUPPOSE* IT'S BETTER THAN CARRYING HER AROUND.

G'WAN, MUN! TELL US SOME *MORE* ABOUT RATS! I WAS *ENJOYIN'* IT!

OH, I DON'T KNOW. WHAT DO YOU WANT?

I COULD TELL YOU ABOUT THE OLD LONDON RATTING PITS. OR ABOUT QUEEN VICTORIA'S RAT-CATCHER, JACK BLACK.

HE'S THE GUY WHO FIRST BRED *FANCY* RATS TO SELL TO LADIES.

OR HOW ABOUT *RAT KINGS?* YOU EVER HEARD OF 'EM?

RAT KINGS?

IT'S *REALLY* STRANGE. SOMETIMES A BUNCH OF RATS GET TOGETHER, BACK TO BACK, AND TIE THEIR TAILS INTO A *KNOT.*

LOOK, YOU CAN SEE ONE IN THIS OLD PRINT.

IT'S ONLY BLACK RATS, *RATTUS RATTUS,* THAT DO THIS.

THEY'RE USUALLY FOUND ALIVE AND THEY'RE NAMED AFTER THE PLACE THEY'RE DISCOVERED— "THE RAT KING OF FRANKFURT" OR BERLIN OR WHEREVER.

Emblen...   ...hes Sambucus (1564). Note the rat k

WEIRD.

THE KNOT IS *UNBREAKABLE.* USUALLY THE BONES OF THE TAIL ARE *CALLOUSED* AND THE ENDS *ATROPHIED.* LOOK AT THE X-RAY.

PERHAPS THEY'RE *BORN* LIKE THAT? GET ALL TIED UP IN THE MOTHER RAT, LIKE.

NO. WHEN THEY'RE BORN THEIR TAILS ARE *TINY.* TOO SMALL TO GET TIED.

BUT WHY DO THEY DO IT, THEN?

NOBODY KNOWS, REALLY. TOTAL MYSTERY.

SOME SAY THEY DO IT TO FORM A SORT OF HYPER-RAT INTELLIGENCE.

FWOAR! RAT KINGS, EH? COOL.

RATS HAVE OPPOSING THUMBS, Y'KNOW. WE'RE DESCENDED FROM SOMETHING LIKE THIS. WHEN...

ER... HELEN?

HMM?

WOULD YOU DO US A FAVOUR? A REAL BIG FAVOUR? I'D REALLY APPRECIATE IT, LIKE.

WHAT?

...UMM... Y'KNOW... Y'KNOW THE GUYS DOWN-STAIRS... WELL,

CAN YOU... ER... IN THE MORNIN', LIKE...

WHAT...?

ER.... ONLY IF THEY ASK, LIKE... COULD YOU SAY, Y'KNOW LIKE, I MEAN, IF THEY ASK...

SAY...?

SAY THAT WE, Y'KNOW... 'AD IT OFF, LIKE, TONIGHT?

HA HA!

YEAH, SURE BEN. NO PROBLEM.

GREAT, MUN, GREAT. THANKS, HELEN, PET. THANKS.

GNORRR

GNORRRRR

PPBBBBBB

PTBBBBBB

WHAT'S UP? DON'T YOU LOVE ME?

'COURSE YOU DO. SO STOP MOANING ABOUT IT.

THIS IS JUST BETWEEN YOU AND ME. YOU MUST *NEVER* TELL ANYBODY. IT'S A SECRET. A PROPER SECRET.

IF YOU TELL ANYBODY YOU'LL BE TAKEN AWAY. YOU DON'T WANT THAT, DO YOU? 'COURSE NOT.

I'M ONLY DOING THIS BECAUSE I *LOVE* YOU. YOU'RE SO PRETTY. MY LITTLE BLONDIE BOMB-SHELL.

C'MON, STOP CRYING PRINCESS.

YOU *DO* WANT TO SHOW ME YOU LOVE ME, DON'T YOU?

DOES THAT FEEL *NICE?*

GOTCHA!

THE LITTLE BITCH WHO STOLE MY ROLEX!

YOU'RE COMING WITH ME TO THE POLICE, MY GEL!

AAARGH!

ROAD

WELL, COME ON! SHOO! SHOO!

RUN FOR IT, YOU STUPID CREATURES!

WELL, WHAT DO YOU WANT?

OH, ALL RIGHT, COME ON' THEN!

ARE YOU ALRIGHT, MISS?

HMM?

ER... YES, THANK YOU. I'M OKAY.

I WAS JUST THINKING OF...ER... I HAD A PET *RAT*. IT JUST *DIED*.

RAT, YOU SAY?

MY COUSIN, HE WAS VERY ILL, YOU KNOW. HE WAS CURED BY RATS.

WHAT?!

OH, YES. HE WENT TO THE *TEMPLE OF RATS* IN NORTH RAJASTHAN. *THOUSANDS* OF RATS ARE LIVING THERE.

PEOPLE TRAVEL SOMETIMES *HUNDREDS* OF MILES TO WORSHIP THEM.

UH OH. HOME TOWN, LITTLE RAT.

YOU CAN SEE OUR TOWER BLOCK.

I'M NEVER GOING BACK.

Y'KNOW, BEATRIX POTTER USED TO TAKE PETER RABBIT— THE *REAL* ONE— ON HOLIDAY WITH HER.

I'VE GOT YOU, EH?

SHE USED TO LOVE GOING ON HOLIDAYS... GETTING AWAY FROM THE CITY...

'SCUSE ME, DARLIN'. THESE SEATS TAKEN?

YES.

SHE DREAMED OF *ESCAPING* INTO A NEW LIFE. ESCAPING FROM THE THIRD FLOOR OF THAT "DARK VICTORIAN MAUSOLEUM" IN BOLTON GARDENS.

AND SHE *DID*.

SHE FINALLY LEFT HER STUPID PARENTS, LEFT *LONDON* AND WENT TO THE *LAKES*.

..."OVER THE HILLS AND FAR AWAY"...

LIKE IN "PIGLING BLAND" AND "THE FAIRY CARAVAN"...

... OFF INTO THE SUNSET, RAT...

... OFF INTO THE SUNSET...

HE'S STOPPING!

HERE WE GO, RATFACE.

SURE! HOP IN, PETAL. I CAN TAKE YOU AS FAR AS AMBLESIDE. I'VE GOT TO DROP SOME STUFF OFF THERE.

...SO I TOLD HIM, SAID STRAIGHT TO HIS FACE, I SAID "THERE'S PLENTY OF JOBS FOR THOSE WHO WANT 'EM". UNEMPLOYMENT? BOLLOCKS. ER, PARDON MY FRENCH...

...TROUBLE IS, THEY'RE FRIGHTENED OF WORK, HALF OF 'EM. YOU GOTTA WORK FOR IT. PUSH YOURSELF. GRASP THE OPPORTUNITIES. THAT'S WHAT ENTERPRISE IS ALL ABOUT. I MEAN TAKE ME...

...SELF-MADE. YOU GOTTA WORK. YOU GOTTA WANT A BETTER WORLD FOR YOURSELF. YOU GOTTA HAVE IMAGINATION.

CAN YOU SEE THAT? DO YOU KNOW WHAT THAT IS ON THE BACK SEAT?

...ER...NO?

IT'S THE FUTURE.

TO BE AN ENTREPRENEUR YOU HAVE TO BE A VISIONARY. YOU HAVE TO SEE HOW TO EXPLOIT THE MARKET, HOW TO STIMULATE AND THEN SUPPLY A DEMAND. IT'S CREATIVE LIKE THAT.

THEY'RE GONNA SELL LIKE HOT CAKES WHEN THE TOURIST SEASON STARTS.

W-WHAT ARE THEY?

THIS IS OUR TURNOFF. I'LL TAKE THE SCENIC ROUTE THROUGH MILNTHORPE AND LEVENS.

THEY'RE HOLOGRAMS, PORTRAITS, SEE. I GET 'EM MADE UP CHEAP IN TAIWAN. LAKE DISTRICT POETS, Y'KNOW, WORDSWORTH, COLERIDGE, DE QUINCEY, SHELLEY... I'M A BLOODY GENIUS, I AM.

CHRIST! WAS THAT NOISE YOUR STOMACH?

MMHM.

ARE YOU OKAY? WHEN WAS THE LAST TIME YOU ATE?

YESTERDAY LUNCHTIME.

I'M JUST TIRED. BEEN HITCHING ALL DAY.

TELL YOU WHAT: WE'LL BE PASSING THE "DAMSON DENE" IN ABOUT FIFTEEN MINUTES. S'A GOOD HOTEL, GOOD FOOD, Y'KNOW, GOOD CUISINE, TOP CLASS.

I'LL BUY YOU A SLAP-UP DINNER. HOW ABOUT THAT, EH?

OH, NO, I COULDN'T...

OH, I INSIST. AND YOU...WELL, YOU CAN PAY ME BACK IN KIND, Y'KNOW, SHOW YOUR GRATITUDE...

...KNOW WHAT I MEAN, LOVE?

AAAAAAH! GET OFF ME!

WHA...

Y-YOU STUPID
LITTLE *SLAG*!

I SHOULD
GET THE *POLICE*
ONTO YOU!

BITCH!
YOU BLOODY
MENACE!

UH...UH...S'LATE, LITTLE RAT...MUST... MUST HAVE BEEN WALKING FOR HOURS...

...LOST...'N' TIRED...'N'...UH...

...DIZZY...'S ALL CATCHING UP WITH ME...

DON'T THINK... I CAN...

UUHHHNN...

...UH...WHU...

...☀...

COUNTRY

SAM, PLEASE, FOR GOD'S SAKE, SAM.

"MR MCGREGOR" ALWAYS MAKES ME THINK OF THAT BLOODY GARDENER IN "PETER RABBIT"!

HEH HEH! M-ME TOO!

YOU HAVE HEARD OF BEATRIX POTTER, THEN?

SHE STOPPED *HERE* ONCE. IN THE '20 S. IN THE ROOM YOU'RE IN AS A MATTER OF FACT.

OH...

SHE WAS CALLED "MRS HEELIS" THEN. SHE WAS HERE WITH HER *HUSBAND*, WATCHING HIM DO HIS *FOLK DANCIN'*, RIGHT HERE ON THE FORECOURT.

THEY LIVED OTHER SIDE OF WINDERMERE AT SAWREY. ANYROAD, WEATHER TURNED BAD AND THEY ENDED UP STAYING THE NIGHT.

OTHER FAMOUS FOLK'VE BEEN HERE...

... WE HAD MERYL STREEP A COUPLE OF YEARS AGO, Y'KNOW.

THE PUB'S IN *"THE SHINING LEVELS"* – JOHN WYATT'S BOOK.

I'LL SHOW IT TO YOU. THERE'S AN ILLUSTRATION OF THE FRONTAGE, DRAWN FROM *OVER THERE* ... ER... ARE YOU OKAY?

OH? MMM. IT'S JUST...ER...BEATRIX POTTER...

WHAT? YOU CAN VISIT HER *HOUSE*, Y'KNOW. "HILL TOP." IT'S OWNED BY THE NATIONAL TRUST...

ER... OH, LOOK. MORE CUSTOMERS. BETTER GET BACK TO WORK.

IT'S A STRANGE FEELING. I'VE COME ALL THIS WAY, FOLLOWED HER FOOTSTEPS... BUT...

...I DON'T WANT TO GO TO HILL TOP. I...I JUST *DON'T*. IT...FRIGHTENS ME. I DON'T FEEL... *READY*, SOMEHOW.

IT'S AS IF... *IF* I WENT THERE I'D HAVE TO FACE... *MYSELF* SOMEHOW... OR... OR...

...OH *I* DON'T KNOW. SOMETHING, NOTHING, I DON'T KNOW.

IT'S JUST ALL *TOO WEIRD*, I MEAN...

...SHE ACTUALLY SLEPT IN *THIS* ROOM, ON THIS BED. ANYHOW...

...LOOKS AS IF WE'LL BE STOPPING HERE FOR A WHILE, LITTLE RAT.

AND, AT THE MOMENT, *ALL* I WANT IS ANOTHER...

MMM. HEAVEN.

UGH. THAT'S HORRIBLE. WHY DO YOU HAVE IT THERE?

"THE SANDY WHISKERED GENTLEMAN"?

OH, THE PUNTERS *LIKE* THAT SORT OF STUFF. IT'S "TRADITIONAL." THEY *EXPECT* IT.

I TEND TO AGREE WITH *OSCAR WILDE.* YOU KNOW, THE BIT ABOUT THE *UNSPEAKABLE* IN PURSUIT OF THE *UNEATABLE.*

YEAH. RIGHT.

THIS IS THE LAKES: *JOHN PEEL* COUNTRY. BLAME IT ON *HIM.* ER... HELEN? ARE YOU OKAY? SETTLING IN?

UH, FINE THANKS.

I...I THOUGHT THAT YOU MIGHT BE...*UPSET* ABOUT SOMETHING. I *DON'T* MEAN TO...

NO, I'M *FINE,* RUTH, HONESTLY. I'VE JUST... HAD SOMETHING ON MY MIND. NOTHING. REALLY.

HMMM. YOU SHOULD GET OUT A BIT. GET SOME FRESH AIR.

YOU SPEND TOO MUCH TIME COOPED UP IN YOUR ROOM.

LOOK, I'LL LEND YOU A MAP IF YOU WANT TO GO WALKABOUT.

WHY, RAVENSBARROW'S ONLY HALF A MILE AWAY...

IS IT THAT *OBVIOUS*, RAT? IT MUST BE WRITTEN ALL OVER MY FACE.

BAD LITTLE GIRL. DIRTY LITTLE BITCH. COMMON AS MUCK.

HMM... THIS WAY.

PERHAPS IT'S NOT *THAT* BAD. PERHAPS I JUST LOOK *PISSED OFF* ALL THE TIME.

I JUST CAN'T SEEM TO GET DAD OUT OF MY HEAD.

LOOK, RAT, MAGPIES. MAGGOTTY PIES... WHAT'S THE *RHYME*...?

ONE FOR SORROW, TWO FOR MIRTH, THREE FOR A WEDDING, FOUR FOR A BIRTH, FIVE FOR SILVER, SIX FOR GOLD...

...SEVEN FOR A SECRET NEVER TO BE TOLD...

...A *SECRET*... NEVER TO BE...

WHOA! NICE VIEW!

LET'S SEE, WHERE ARE WE?

WELL...THE SEA OVER THERE, THAT'S MORECAMBE BAY...

THAT RIDGE JUST OPPOSITE IS WHITBARROW SCAR...THAT ONE'S SCOUT SCAR... KENDAL'S JUST BEHIND IT...

...THERE'S THE WINSTER WINDING THROUGH THE VALLEY...

...HM. THAT MUST BE CARTMEL FELL CHURCH DOWN THERE. LET'S CHECK IT OUT.

...EIGHT FOR HEAVEN, NINE FOR HELL...

...AND TEN FOR THE DIVIL'S OWN SEL'.

CERTAINLY SECLUDED HERE, FAT RAT.

PEACEFUL. LIKE THE EYE IN THE MIDDLE OF A HURRICANE...

"UNDERNEATH THIS STONE A MOULD'RING VIRGIN LIES WHO WAS THE PLEASURE ONCE OF HUMAN EYES..."?

UGH! THAT'S GROSS!

THAT'S ME, RAT...

...A MOULDERING VIRGIN.

AYE, IT ALWAYS AMAZES ME TOO. THE TOURIST TRAPS ARE PACKED LIKE *SARDINE TINS* WHILE THE FELLS ARE *EMPTY.* IT'S *LUDICROUS.*

WHAT'S THE BEST WAY TO TRAVEL ABOUT? ARE THERE *BUSES* UP HERE OR WHAT?

UP HERE? HA HA HA!

YOU HAVE TO CATCH A MOUNTAIN GOAT!

"THERE'S A STRENGTH THAT COMES FROM THESE HILLS."

SHE FELL IN LOVE WITH THIS LAND. I CAN SEE WHY.

SHEEE! I THOUGHT THE BUGGERS'D *NEVER* LEAVE TONIGHT! HELEN, PULL ME A PINT, WOULD YOU LOVE?

ACTUALLY, YOU CAN PULL US ALL ONE.

SEE HOW BUSY IT IS ONCE THE SEASON GETS GOING? I'M *EXHAUSTED*.

TA. I NEED THIS.

HAVE YOU THOUGHT ANY MORE ON WHAT WE WERE SAYIN'?

ER...YES, I HAVE. I- I'VE NOT *DECIDED* YET.

IT'S *GREAT* OF YOU AND RUTH TO OFFER ME A *PERMANENT* PLACE HERE. REALLY GREAT.

I'LL LET YOU KNOW VERY SOON.

I WAS REALLY DEAD LUCKY TO MEET YOU AT ALL. I... I DON'T KNOW *WHAT* WOULD'VE HAPPENED IF I HADN'T ENDED UP HERE.

WE'RE THE LUCKY ONES, HELEN.

WE USUALLY TAKE ON KIDS FROM THE LOCAL FARMS. THEY DON'T LIVE HERE IN THE PUB, LIKE YOU. I MEAN, THEY HAVE THEIR OWN FAMILIES, AND WE ENJOY, I MEAN, WE LIKE HAVING YOU AROUND, I MEAN ...

WHAT SHE MEANS IS...

... WE NEVER HAD ANY CHILDREN OF OUR OWN, AND WE KIND OF...

AAAH!

MORNING, HELEN. ARE ... ARE YOU OKAY?

GOING DOWN TO BOWLAND BRIDGE ... POSTING A LETTER ...

... TO MY PARENTS. THEY ... THEY DON'T KNOW WHERE I AM, RUTH.

I'VE ASKED THEM TO PHONE ME HERE.

HELEN, WE'VE NEVER ASKED ABOUT ... WE ... WELL, WE DON'T WANT TO BE NOSY. IT'S YOUR PRIVATE BUSINESS. BUT ...

... LOOK, WHY DON'T YOU INVITE THEM HERE? THEY CAN STOP THE NIGHT IF YOU LIKE. YOU CAN SHOW THEM THAT YOU'RE SOMEWHERE SAFE.

WE ... WE KNOW YOU'VE BEEN UPSET ABOUT SOMETHING. WE CAN SEE HOW SAD YOU'VE BEEN. YOU KNOW ...

... DEPRESSION IS OFTEN ANGER TURNED INWARDS.

DON'T BOTTLE IT UP. YOU HAVE TO EXPRESS IT. JUST LET IT ALL OUT.

I KNOW. I'M PLANNING ON IT.

WILL YOU WALK TO THE VILLAGE WITH ME?

RUTH, ABOUT LAST NIGHT. I'M REALLY SORRY...

NO NEED TO BE. IT'S ALL RIGHT, HONESTLY.

NO, IT'S NOT. IT'S NOT ALL RIGHT. IT'S PATHETIC. I'M PATHETIC.

BUT I'M GOING TO CHANGE. IF SHE COULD CHANGE, THEN I CAN CHANGE.

WHO...?

BEATRIX POTTER.

"PAINFULLY SHY" SHE WAS, BUT SHE EVENTUALLY STOOD UP TO HER PARENTS, HER FATHER.

THAT'S WHAT I HAVE TO DO.

THE PSYCHOTHERAPY BOOKS ALL SAY SO. CONFRONTING THE ABUSER IS A MAJOR PART OF THE HEALING PROCESS.

ABUSER? OH MY GOD. YOU POOR GIRL.

THE WORST THING IS THAT I CAN'T GET IT OUT OF MY HEAD FOR MORE THAN A FEW MINUTES AT A TIME. I CAN'T. I RECALL THINGS, I SEE THINGS SO CLEARLY, SO VIVIDLY.

IT'S A CURSE. RUTH ...

YES?

...I DO NEED SOME HELP WITH THIS.

I NEED TO TALK IT THROUGH. I NEED SOMEONE TO LISTEN.

YOU DON'T HAVE TO ASK. I'M HERE, HELEN. WE HAVE A FEW DAYS AT LEAST.

DON'T YOU CHANGE TOO MUCH. FROM WHAT I REMEMBER, BEATRIX POTTER BECAME A RIGHT OLD BOOT: TOUGH AS NAILS.

HA HA! THAT'S RIGHT! YOU KNOW, TRAMPS USED TO THINK THAT SHE WAS ONE OF THEM!

MORE THAN THAT, SHE BECAME A REAL COUNTRY-WOMAN.

"ONE PLACE SUITS ONE PERSON, ANOTHER PLACE SUITS ANOTHER PERSON."

THAT'S FROM HER STORY OF THE TOWN MOUSE AND THE COUNTRY MOUSE.

THIS PLACE SUITED HER ...

... SUITS ME TOO.

AND NOBODY'S GOING TO TAKE IT AWAY FROM ME.

...SO HE SAYS TO HIM, HE SAYS "ARE YOU *SHEARIN'* IT?", HA-HA, AND THE *FARMER* GOES "NO! SOD OFF AN' *CATCH YOUR OWN!*", HA-HA!

GET IT? HA-HA-HA!

REALLY! WE DON'T WANT TO HEAR STUFF LIKE THAT *HERE*, NORMAN.

GET AWAY WITH YOU.

WELL, MR...ER, SAM, THAT WAS THE *BEST PUB* LUNCH I'VE HAD FOR AGES. LOVELY.

AND THANKS FOR LOOKING AFTER OUR DAUGHTER. YOU KNOW WE HAD THE *POLICE* LOOKING FOR HER? WE WERE WORRIED SICK.

SHE'S BEEN A SILLY, NAUGHTY GIRL. I *DON'T KNOW.* YOU BRING 'EM UP AN' EVERYTHING AND *THIS* IS THE *THANKS* YOU GET.

ANYROAD, SHE'LL BE OFF YOUR HANDS *TOMORROW* WHEN WE GO BACK HOME.

WHAT?

YOU'RE WRONG THERE, DAD. I'M *STOPPING.*

RUTH AND SAM HAVE OFFERED ME A PERMANENT JOB HERE, AND I'VE *ACCEPTED.*

NOW WAIT JUST A BLOODY MINUTE...

FATHER.

I WANT TO TALK TO YOU IN PRIVATE. PLEASE FOLLOW ME.

HELEN...?

WELL! SHE'S NEVER CALLED HIM "FATHER" BEFORE.

CHEEKY LITTLE MONKEY.

ER ... 'SCUSE ME, THAT T-SHIRT, WHAT...?

EH?

OH, RAT KINGS? YEAH, GOOD BAND. THEY'VE BEEN DOIN' THE LONDON PUB CIRCUIT. GETTIN' BIG. I'VE SEEN 'EM.

RAT KINGS

SINGER'S THIS LANKY GEORDIE BLOKE WITH GLASSES...

HA-HA-HA!

...EH?

WHAT'S WITH HER?

HA-HA-HA!

HEH...WHOA!

THE ...THE STARS...

...SO CLEAR...

IT'S *INCREDIBLE*, RAT. AND IT'S STARTED SINCE I CONFRONTED DAD.

AND SAYING IT ALL TO HIM, GETTING IT OFF MY CHEST, ALL THE THINGS THAT I'VE WANTED TO TELL HIM...

NOW ALL THAT STUFF ISN'T ON MY MIND *ALL THE TIME*, IT'S SORT OF OPENED THINGS UP, FREED MY *THOUGHTS*.

I'VE BEGUN TO HAVE LOTS OF GREAT IDEAS FOR *STORIES*...

... AND *PICTURES*, TOO. THE "VISIONS" AREN'T A *CURSE*. THEY'RE A *TALENT*, A BLESSING REALLY.

BEATRIX POTTER HAD IT, A VIVID, VISUAL IMAGINATION. WHAT SHE CALLED "*THE SEEING EYE.*" TAKE YOU, FOR INSTANCE...

... I CAN SEE YOU DOWN TO YOUR LAST WHISKER...

HMMM. EVER HEARD OF *HARVEY*?

THAT'S THE PUB IN "JEMIMA PUDDLEDUCK."

LOOK RAT.

AND OVER THERE'S CASTLE COTTAGE WHERE POTTER LIVED AFTER SHE GOT MARRIED.

ONCE upon a time, there was a very bad rat.

Her name was Helen Barnrat. She knew that she must be a very bad rat because everybody told her so; Mr. and Mrs. Barnrat were constantly chastising her, and her teacher was cross because she always came bottom of the class.

One morning, she awoke to bright sunshine and the sound of throstles singing. Oh, what a yawny — stretchy rat that was!

All at once — she realized she had overslept!

SHE jumped out of bed and scurried to the living room. She was late for Rat School!

"Oh, why did I oversleep?" she cried. But she knew perfectly well.

Every night, Mr. Barnrat told Helen that if she did not behave herself, Owd Scratch would come and get her.

Owd Scratch was a notorious cat; a cat to be feared. He was a huge, one-eyed, mangy cat of many winters and a ferocious ratter.

She had heard the rhyme:

"Not last night, but the night before,
A big, fat tomcat came knocking at my door.
'I'm OWD SCRATCH,' he said to me,
'And I eat rats like thee for tea!'"

AND that was why Helen had overslept. She had been so frightened of the horrid Owd Scratch that she had been quite unable to get to sleep for most of the night.

Helen was in a fearful pickle. And she was so busy thinking about Owd Scratch that — BUMP! — she ran straight into Mrs. Barnrat.

"Oh, my whiskers!" her Mother exclaimed, dropping all the breakfast crockery. It fell with a SMASH! CRASH! TINKLE! CRASH!

Her Father, who had been quietly lighting a pipeful of rat-tobacco, was so surprised at the noise that he jumped up, burning his nose. "YOCK! YOCK! EEK!" he squeaked loudly.

MR. and Mrs. Barnrat were exceedingly annoyed.

"You bad little rat! You bad little rat!" her Mother scolded. "What a nasty little rat you are," said her Father, grinding his teeth.

This made Helen cry.

"Now go and get ready for school!" they squeaked. "No breakfast for you today!"

But when Helen went back to her room, do you know what she did? She did not get ready for school!

INSTEAD, she packed up her favourite books, some sunflower seeds, her acorn-cup, her toothbrush, her tortoiseshell hairbrush, some pine-needle pins, and her life's savings, which amounted to five peppercorns.

"I've had enough of this," she thought. "I'm going to run away from home, and BOTHER school!"

What a naughty, bad rat!

Then she sneaked out of her room, around a hay-bale, along a beanpole, down a stove-pipe, behind some rolls of old oilcloth, out of the barn (by way of her secret trapdoor), and pitter-pattered away down Toad Road.

IT was a beautiful, sunny day; Red Admiral and Peacock butterflies danced in the air, and somewhere a Yellowhammer was singing "A little bit of bread and NO CHEESE! A little bit of bread and NO CHEESE!"

Helen Barnrat followed Toad Road to the top of Cuckoo Brow, then turned to look back. She could see the rooftops of the farm where she had lived for all of her short life, and she felt sad.

"I wish I wasn't such a bad rat," she said to herself. "I don't want to leave home, but I cannot bear it anymore; I really can't stay. I must go over the hills and far away."

And with that, Helen descended the far side of Cuckoo Brow.

S HE was passing through a copse and starting to feel hungry when... Crack! The sudden snap of a breaking twig made her scramble for cover. And not a second too soon, for as she crouched beneath an old oak fern, a hunter appeared, sniffing the air.

All Helen could do was hold her breath, stay perfectly still, and hope that the sandy-whiskered squire would quickly pass by.

T HEN she nearly jumped out of her skin! For a voice behind her hissed — "Pssst! Little Rat!"

"Pssst!" It went again, "Over here!" And looking around, Helen could see a pair of black eyes twinkling at her from inside a hole in the bank.

The voice and the eyes seemed friendly and so, with a springy bound, Helen dived into the safety of the tunnel.

PRESENTLY, a soft light spread all around her as the occupant struck a lucifer and lit an oil lamp. Helen could now see that he was a spiny hedgehog and that she was in the hedgehog's home.

"Snuff! Pleased to meet you, Little Rat," he said, "Urchin Leafmould at your service. Absolutely! I was just about to commence lunch and it would give me great pleasure if you joined me in some raspberries. Snuff, snuff, snuff!"

HELEN politely accepted, although she was rather in awe of this prickly stranger. She was treated to some delicious raspberries in honeydew, but respectfully declined to partake of some horrid-looking ragworms, earwigs, and woodlice in slug sauce.

"So, Longtail, tell me — snuff — why did you run away from home?" asked Urchin Leafmould, crunching an earwig's leg.

Helen explained how she was so terrified at the thought of Owd Scratch that she could do nothing right.

"At home I can think of nothing else," — she squeaked. "My father threatens me with that cat nonstop. So I'm going where there are lots of other rats. My Aunt Janie lives at Hill Top Farm. I can stay with her."

Urchin Leafmould was very sympathetic in his snuffly way, and after lunch he showed Helen the path to Hill Top.

"OH, it's terribly, terribly close," he snuffled. "Absolutely! Just over there past the cow parsley, snuff, hemlock, snuff, jack-by-the-hedge, snuff, sweet cicely, snuff, hog-weed, snuff, and other assorted umbelliferie. But before you depart, Little Rat, please take the advice that I now — snuff — will freely offer."

The hedgehog wrinkled his nose and looked up at the racing clouds far overhead. "I ran away from home, when I was young you know. Oh, absolutely! For years I was a proper urchin! And there's something that I learned about — snuff — cats."

"There is one thing that cats will never do. And do you know — snuff — what that thing is?" he looked at her sharply, his black eyes glittering.

"I can't imagine!" said Helen.

"What they are told! Absolutely! No cat will ever do what it is told! Snuff, snuff, snuff!"

He seemed to think this tremendously funny.

And even when Helen had taken her leave and turned to wave back at him, Urchin Leafmould was still shaking with unbounded amusement.

BUT he was right about one thing; Hill Top was "terribly close," and after ten scampering minutes she arrived.

Now Hill Top Farm is where I live. And let me tell you, it was completely infested by rats. I had no end of trouble with them! But recently things had changed...

Helen Barnrat pitter-pattered across the farmyard feeling very self-conscious. Cows watched her, pigs watched her, the chickens watched her — but there was not another rat to be seen. Where on earth could they be?

Then she saw something that made her blood turn to ice. Nailed to the cowshed door were dozens and dozens of rats' tails! No rats, only the tails nailed there like trophies!

At that moment, a dark shadow fell across Helen and she smelt a smelly, fusky, musky, catty smell that made her eyes water.

"HOW now, a RAT?" a deep voice growled behind her. "Dead for a ducat, DEAD! Ha-ha-ha!"

It was none other than Owd Scratch himself.

Helen looked up, trembling. She was so dreadfully frightened that she durst not move.

"Such a leetle rat!" exclaimed Owd Scratch. "A gay young frisker! Yum yum!"

Helen was horrified — with popping eyes she saw the ugly gralloching knife in the cat's belt and the bird and rat skulls hanging around his neck.

Owd Scratch did not live at Hill Top. He had come to the farm as a hireling ratter after hearing of its enormous rat population.

CAT fleas squirmed under his stained mouseskin coat. He licked his lips with his rough cat tongue. "My favourite dish, with the possible exception of mouse sausages and tripe, is young rat-attouie!" he grinned. "An excellent starter!"

Now, it is contrary to rat nature to be able to think clearly in the presence of cats, but Helen tried to do her best in the circumstances.

"P-p-please, sir," she said, quaking with fear, "p-p-please don't eat me. I c-can pay you."

Helen opened the kerchief containing her few possessions. "H-h-here are f-f-five p-p-pepper-corns," she offered, laying them on the ground before the huge, old tom.

He snatched them up and tipped them into his purse. "What a foolish leetle rat," he laughed, "to think that you could bribe Owd Scratch! Money for nowt! Money for nowt! Ha-ha-ha!"

"DON'T you know," he sneered, baring his frightful teeth, "that I am the cat that killed the rat that ate the malt that lay in the house that Jack built? And now it is your turn!"

He flexed his cruel claws and drew them along the ground — scr-r-itch, scratch, scrit! Scr-r-itch, scratch, scrit!

Then he arched his back and bent down so close to the transfixed rat that she felt his hot cat breath on her face. She winced at his fat-cat halitosis.

36

37

ALL at once a queer thing happened. Helen thought to herself — "Why, he's nothing but a mangy, moggy BULLY!" And with one quick swipe she scratched his single eye with her sharp little nails.

"MEOOOW!" screamed Owd Scratch, "MEOOOW!"

He held up a paw to his eye and snarled and spat at her. "You vicious little rat!" he shrieked, stumbling toward her and clawing the air with his free paw. "Just you wait! I'll get you for that, even if you do escape me now. I'm the best ratter there is!"

"That's all flummery," said Helen calmly. "If you think I'm going to take to my heels now, then you're very much mistaken."

38

39

THIS infuriated Owd Scratch. "Little rubbish! Little rubbish!" he spat. "Where are you?"

"Right here!" Helen said. "TAKE THREE STEPS FORWARD!"

Of course, cats being contrary, Owd Scratch immediately took three steps backwards. His third step sent him tripping over a low stone wall, whereupon with a cat-aclysmic, cat-astrophic, cat-awauling, he plunged straight down the shaft of the Hill Top well!

BEFORE Helen knew what was happening, hundreds of rats appeared; from under the chicken coop, from lumber, from over bales and under, singing: "Ding-dong bell! Pussy's in the well!" (They must have been watching all the time.)

They bore Helen up on their shoulders and proclaimed her a brave rat, a good rat, a great rat, the best rat in the world!

IT was at this point that I heard their squeaking and marched into the farmyard with a broom. All the rats scuttled away but one; Helen Barnrat looked up at me, sniffing. I suppose that having seen off Owd Scratch, she was not going to be intimidated merely by one of the Big Folk who smelled of sheep!

I couldn't bring myself to hurt this brave little rat, so instead, I went to fish the humiliated tomcat, who was mewing piteously, out of the well.

Owd Scratch, now a bedraggled soggy moggy, slunk away in shame, never to be seen around Sawrey again.

AND as for Helen Barnrat?

Well, now that she was no longer terrified of Owd Scratch, she realized that she was a very good rat indeed!

The Congress of Rats awarded her the "Freedom of the Farmyard" and an annual income of one hundred peppercorns for ridding them of the N.C. (Nasty Cat).

She wrote and drew a story about her experience and called it *The Tale of One Bad Rat*. It was sold in the village store and become a rat best-seller. So from being a common, or garden, rat Helen became an uncommonly famous rat.

And now she is a perfectly contented rat. She writes rat stories, paints rat pictures, and...

...she is never bothered by cats!

THE END

...ESCAPING THE *REPRESSIVE* ATMOSPHERE OF HER *CHILDHOOD.* HER FATHER, *RUPERT POTTER,* WAS A KEEN...

...AND HE EVEN *REFUSED* TO ALLOW MILLAIS TO PAINT HER *PORTRAIT* BECAUSE HE *THOUGHT* THAT IT WOULD MAKE HER *VAIN*...

RAT'S TAIL

ONCE upon a time, I had the notion to write and draw a story about the English Lake District.

I'd been in love with the place since I was fourteen, when my parents bought a "static caravan" on a trailer park in the Winster Valley for holidays and weekends. On the days when we weren't motoring around the beauty spots and tourist magnets, I spent hours exploring the immediate area; Bowland Bridge, Strawberry Bank, Ravensbarrow, and Cartmel Fell are all there as depicted in *The Tale of One Bad Rat*.

I could have produced a documentary comic book. There's certainly no lack of material. The Lake District has the widest range of geological features and types of scenery in such a small area in the world. Wordsworth's "beauty lying in the lap of horror" — its lush valleys and spectacular crags — were an inspiration to the English Romantic Movement. Samuel Taylor Coleridge, writer of the *Ancient Mariner*, invented the sport of rock climbing there. Dr. Johnson, Shelley, Dickens, Ruskin, Turner, and many others all have connections with the area. Then there's the huntsman, John Peel; writer Arthur Ransome; film star Stan Laurel; Donald Campbell, who crashed whilst attempting to break his world water speed record on Coniston; and Canon Hardwicke Rawnsley, poet, co-founder of the National Trust and friend of the family of the young Beatrix Potter.

Now, Beatrix Potter — an expert at telling stories using a combination of words and pictures — *there* was a correlation with comic art. Being unfamiliar with her work, I began to research, starting with Margaret Lane's *The Tale of Beatrix Potter* and a visit to Hill Top. However, I didn't want to do a biography; I was just looking for a way in.

Potter was an oppressed child. Starved of affection, not sent to school, she was kept a virtual prisoner on the third story of the family house. As a young girl, she was "unnaturally lonely," "exceedingly shy and tongue-tied" in company, and her only true friends were the small animals she accumulated, studied, and drew.

I was reminded of a teen-age girl I'd seen begging on a platform of Tottenham Court Road tube station. She looked excruciatingly shy and was being hassled by a huge, bearded Jesus freak . . .

The rat theme seemed natural for it. We'd had a pet rat ever since my son Alwyn had pestered us into getting him one. Harpo was so intelligent that he immediately became the family pet. (There's a photograph of him on my shoulder in *The Adventures of Luther Arkwright* #10, Valkyrie edition.) Beatrix Potter had a pet rat, famous through the dedication in her "rat book" *The Tale of Samuel Whiskers*; "In remembrance of 'Sammy,' the intelligent, pink-eyed representative of a persecuted (but irrepressible) race. An affectionate litle friend, and most accomplished thief." And *The Tale of One Bad Rat* sounded exactly like a Potter story.

Producing a proposal for the story with a color cover illustration based on my recollection of the girl at the tube station, I sent a copy to every publisher of illustrated books in Britain. It occurred to me that,

Helen Beatrix Potter, 1866-1943, age 16

Kate Housden

since the story was non-genre, it had the potential to have a mainstream readership. These were all returned, mostly by return of post, mostly unread. The submission editors had reached the words "graphic novel" or "comics" in the cover letter and cut off.

I did receive offers from comics companies. Michael Bennent, then editor for Dark Horse UK, liked the concept, and we had a meeting with publisher Mike Richardson at the Alexandra Palace Comic Convention. I'd worked with Dark Horse before and had a good working relationship with them. Mike gave me the go-ahead.

At that time, I was right in the middle of writing and drawing a Batman story for DC Comics and so *Bad Rat* had to wait. And I still had lots of research to do. By this point, I'd read a few books on the Lake District, four about rats, and approximately a dozen on Beatrix Potter. It was time to have a look at sexual abuse . . .

When putting together the proposal, I'd worked on the basic premise: a homeless girl with a synchronistic link with Beatrix Potter follows Potter's escape into her new life in the Lakes. The plot demanded a reason for her leaving home. Without much consideration, I keyed in "fleeing sexual abuse at the hands of her father." It was glib but, I thought, a pretty reasonable plot device. After all, it's one of the most common causes of teen-age homelessness. And it seemed to fit the character of the shy protagonist.

I read over a dozen books on the sexual abuse of children and its effect on psychological development. In fact, one book would have done. The same sort of coercion, an emotional blackmail, takes place; and the same results, the behavioral symptoms, recur with monotonous regularity. Reading transcripts of accounts by sexual abuse victims, even by those from different countries, you'll find the same situations described and the same feelings paraphrased. The utter selfishness of the abuser is the common denominator — not class, race, or creed. The psychological aftereffects — despair and withdrawal; low self-esteem; feeling worthless, dirty and bad — can last for life. The children take the badness onto themselves.

It's been estimated that one in three girls will be molested before they're eighteen. Approximately 90% of that abuse is committed, not by the stereotypical stranger in the raincoat, haunter of the schoolgates, but by a close, male relative.

Ben Evans

Keith Marsland

story and used some of the methods of Frank Hampson: a mixture of invention, photo reference, and life drawing.

Within a week of having to start pencilling, I still hadn't found the model for Helen. Invited to give a lecture on comics art at a local college, I mentioned this to the organiser, Peter Hartley, head of drama. By the time of the lecture, Peter had three of his students lined up to audition for the role. I was astounded. There was Helen, as I had imagined her, in the person of Kate Housden. Kate was indispensable to this project. As I was telling Kate about *Bad Rat*, Ben — as described in detail in the script — walked past. I told him about the Ben character. "I'll pose," he said, "That's my name!"

The location shots I did over a couple of years, sometimes having to stop drawing to take the train to London or drive to Cumbria because I didn't have the correct reference. I followed Helen's walk from Chelsea to Kensington to the site of Beatrix Potter's natal home in Bolton Gardens, bombed during the London blitz. Like Potter, I occasionally resorted to

And less than one in twenty of reported offenders are prosecuted.

This issue was far too important to marginalize; I needed to change the nature of the story in order to address it. It became *Bad Rat*'s raison d'être and the chief concern of the plot.

The story dictated the illustration technique. This is true for every comic I've worked on; I've always tried to adapt my drawing style to project the different atmospheres required by each individual story. With *Bad Rat*, this meant a drastic stylistic change. Because of the content and the mainstream nature of the story, I felt that it needed to be clear and accessible, easily readable by those without an acquired knowledge of comics grammar.

Usually I "create on the page." Working in the genres of science-fiction or superhero adventure comics, it's perfectly acceptable to make up characters and landscapes. I felt very strongly that I had to ground *Bad Rat* firmly in reality, basing all the characters on real people and all the scenes on real locations. I carefully cast the

Preparatory pencil study of dead rat

Bryan Talbot outside the Mason's Arms

artistic licence to "improve" the composition of some of the Lake District scenes, although the majority are faithful renditions. In answer to several queries, the view at the beginning and end of the book is of Crummock Water and Buttermere, from just below Haystacks.

Sometimes stories really do take on a life of their own. Instead of creating a comic about the Lake District, I ended up writing and drawing a story about child sexual abuse. And I'm glad it turned out that way. This has been the most worthwhile book that I have been involved with and the best — not to mention the hardest — comics work that I've ever done.

Worthwhile?

"The first step towards prevention and to provision of supportive services for the girls who've been abused is bringing abuse into the open . . . Incest is not taboo. It seems to be that talking about incest is the real taboo." Miriam Saphira, *The Sexual Abuse of Children*.

It's only recently that abuse has been openly discussed in some small way in the media, and there's a backlash of opinion about even this. People don't want to hear it, don't want to have to think about it. I can only think of three, perhaps four, examples in the comic-book medium that have ever tried to deal with it, even in passing. This backlash is often expressed in dismissive terms, as if we all know about the subject now and there's no point bringing it up

again. Sexual abuse occurs a great deal more frequently than murder, but watch television for a night, pick up a novel, go to the cinema, and what do you see? But then, talking about murder is not taboo.

The fact is, because the media largely ignores it, this abuse can still go on unhindered. It works in a conspiracy of silence. Most of the victims, the younger the more likely, believe that this frightening, confusing thing is happening to them alone. They dare not talk about it to anyone and become lonely and alienated. Read Helen's dialogue concerning her feelings. This was paraphrased from transcripts of interviews with abuse survivors. I tried to let the victims speak for themselves.

The more child abuse is discussed in society or fiction in whatever medium, the more likely it is that the victims will realise that it is something that happens all the time, that they can speak out, be believed, and get it stopped.

BRYAN TALBOT
Lancashire, England
May 1995

Bryan Talbot at the porch, Hill Top

ACKNOWLEDGMENTS

TO the following writers and artists for comment and encouragement on the work in progress: Leo Baxendale, Ramsey Campbell, John Coulthart, Al Davison, Glenn Fabry, Ben Hunt, Neil Gaiman, Stephen Gallagher, Colin Greenland, Gwyneth Jones, Steve Leialoha, Alan Moore, Eric Pringle, Roger Sabin, Dave Sim, Trina Robbins, Mary Talbot, and Tom Veitch.

To the abuse survivors who talked to me, for information, comment, and letting me know that I was getting it right.

To the London Metropolitan Police (Thames Division, Waterloo Pier), Stuart Mason (art teacher at Tulketh High School, Preston), Dick Hansom, and Dick Jude for help with location shots.

To Dave Frost, the late Frank McConville, (Scouse advisors), Al Davison, and Chris Moir (Geordie advisors).

To hairdresser Robin Simmons of Preston for calculating the monthly growth rate of Helen's hair.

To Pip and Julie Grundy and James and Pauline Brunton, cat wranglers.

To Nigel and Helen Stevenson, proprietors of The Mason's Arms, Crosthwaite, the real-life Herdwick Arms for allowing their pub to be used as a backdrop.

To Judy Taylor, author of *Beatrix Potter, Artist, Storyteller and Countrywoman* and Chair of the Beatrix Potter Society, for championing *The Tale of One Bad Rat*.

And to my models: Pete Applegarth; Krishnan Arya; James Barker; Benjamin Blackledge; Theresa Bond; Babu Chauhan; Jean Dixon; Ben Evans; Clair Flannery; Ellen, Marilyn, and Steve Gallagher; Sid Heathcote; Graham Holland; Kate Housden; Graeme Hurry; Les Isbister; Frank McConville; Keith and Sarita Marsland; Nick Robinson; Gary and Hilary Smith; Joan Smith; Jane Sorenson; Alwyn, Mary, and Robin Talbot; and Neil Wheeler.

The rats: Harpo, Vasquez, Daisy, Mad Mink Mortimer, and Beatrix.

B RYAN Talbot has worked in underground comics, such as *Knockabout*, *Slow Death*, and *Brainstorm*. He produced SF humour strips *Frank Fazakerly, Space Ace of the Future* for *Ad Astra* and *Scumworld* for *Sounds*.

First serialized in *Near Myths* and *Pssst!* magazine, his award-winning story, the seminal *The Adventures of Luther Arkwright*, begun in 1978, was the hugely influential first British graphic novel and is now available in one volume from Dark Horse Comics.

Bryan worked for the British SF weekly comic *2000AD* on *Nemesis the Warlock* and *Judge Dredd*, and for DC Comics drawing *The Nazz*, *Hellblazer*, *Sandman*, *Dead Boy Detectives*, *Fables*, and the Paradox Big Books, and writing and drawing *The Dreaming* and *Legends of the Dark Knight*. He also wrote and drew *Neil Gaiman's Teknophage* for *Tekno Comics*.

The Tale of One Bad Rat is published in nine countries and has won numerous international awards. It featured in the *New York Times* annual list of recommended reading and is used as a resource in schools and child abuse centres in several countries.

His most recent graphic novel is the parallel world historical fantasy epic *Heart of Empire*, published by Dark Horse. He is currently writing and drawing the "dream documentary" of Lewis Carroll, *Alice in Sunderland*.

His website is at http://www.bryan-talbot.com

NEED help or counseling or know someone who does? These help lines are toll-free:

Within the U.K., call
Childline at 0800 1111

Within the U.S.A., call
Childhelp at 1-800-422-4453

Within Canada, call
Kids Help Phone 1-800-668-6868